# We're going on a TREASURE HUNT

Words by

*Martha Mumford*

Illustrated by

*Laura Hughes*

BLOOMSBURY
CHILDREN'S BOOKS
LONDON  OXFORD  NEW YORK  NEW DELHI  SYDNEY

We're going on a treasure hunt.
# YO! HO! HO!
Help us find the golden coins . . .

We're going on a treasure hunt.
Splash, splosh, splish.
Watch out for the
DOLPHINS . . .

We're going on a treasure hunt.
YO! HO! HO!
Help us find the golden coins . . .

We're going on a treasure hunt.

Drip, drop, drip.

Watch out for the

CRABS . . .

We're going on a treasure hunt.
Ooo-ooo-ooo!
Watch out for the
MONKEYS...

We're going on a treasure hunt.

YO! HO! HO!

Help us find the golden coins . . .

We're going on a treasure hunt.
Squawk, squawk, screech.
Watch out for the
PARROTS...

Look –
another
beach!

We're going on a treasure hunt.
YO! HO! HO!
Help us find the golden coins . . .

Quick, quick, crabs –

Snip, snap, snip!

Quick, quick, dolphins –

Swoosh, swoosh, swish!

Quick, quick, little buns – *go, go, go!*

Land ahoy!

Back home at last.

That adventure was

THE BEST!

But there's one last thing to FIND . . .

*For Annie and Jeff x – L.H.*

BLOOMSBURY CHILDREN'S BOOKS
Bloomsbury Publishing Plc
50 Bedford Square, London, WC1B 3DP, UK

BLOOMSBURY, BLOOMSBURY CHILDREN'S BOOKS and the Diana logo are trademarks of Bloomsbury Publishing Plc
First published in Great Britain 2020 by Bloomsbury Publishing Plc
Text copyright © Bloomsbury Publishing Plc, 2020
Illustrations copyright © Laura Hughes, 2020

Laura Hughes has asserted her right under the Copyright, Designs and Patents Act, 1988, to be identified as Illustrator of this work

A catalogue record for this book is available from the British Library

ISBN: HB: 978-1-4088-9340-1
PB: 978-1-4088-9339-5

2 4 6 8 10 9 7 5 3 1 (hardback)
2 4 6 8 10 9 7 5 3 1 (paperback)

Printed and bound in China by Leo Paper Products, Heshan, Guangdong
All papers used by Bloomsbury Publishing Plc are natural, recyclable products from wood grown in well managed forests.
The manufacturing processes conform to the environmental regulations of the country of origin

To find out more about our authors and books visit www.bloomsbury.com and sign up for our newsletters